Jyoti Patel

The Mystic Soul

I would like to dedicate this book to the love of my life, my parents, my brother and to you, my reader.
My passion towards writing will always be a burning flame of my life. I want to reach as many people as I can through my words.
I would like to thank all those who read my works and appreciated, also the people who criticized and tried to pull me back.
My heartfelt thanks to all my readers for their boundless love and encouragement, those who are connected to me on the social media.
You all mean a lot to me. I hope this book ***The Mystic Soul*** gives you the noble warmth of feeling, spirit and courage.

Table of contents.

1. My little angel.

She always know,
Just what to say.
Just talking to her,
Makes my day.

Not caring what's ahead,
We're madly in love.
She takes me to a place,
Where I will always be safe.
Words can't describe,
How I feel about her
My little angel, she is.

2. Together and forever.

I love you honey with all of my heart,
Together forever and never to part.

You are the sun that shines bright,
You are the moon that shimmers.

You are the gravity that holds me,
You are stars that glimmer.

I see you in my thoughts and dreams,
I see you every second of life.

I see you standing next to me,
I can feel you with all my heart.

I feel your warmth at my side,
The pain in my heart
moves to my eyes each night.

You are the one I need,
You are the one I want, though
You aren't here to comfort me,
But soon I hope you will be.

3. Feelings.

The first hand I held,
The first one I cared for.

The first lips I touched,
The only one I ever loved.

We made it happen,
After a long wait, I held you tight.
We weren't allowed to talk,
But still, we managed.
I held you so tight,
I didn't want to let go.

You were the first one I ever cried for,
Besides my daddy when he left me.

I remember the way you caressed me,
I can always feel your hands over mine.

The feelings I feel for you,
I'm never letting them go.

4. The time will amend.

Lost is the guy
With the lonely heart,
A girl, waiting for her love
With a long and weary smile.

She stole his heart,
Before he'd even seen.

She'd be his princess,
And he'd be her prince,
Though far away.
He was born to love her
All of his life.
He knows in his heart,
A connection between them
Cannot be torn apart.

She awaits his return,
Love brought them near,
And will see them to the end.
Together they'll be,
Their distance, the time will amend.

5. I knew...

I knew from the moment I saw you,
That you would be worth every lonely night
I'd have to spend without you.

For the first time,
When I looked into your eyes,
I saw the belief you had on me.

When I touched your hand for the first time,
I felt the trust you had on me.

When I walk with you,
I feel my journey to be complete.

When I hug you close to my heart,
I can listen to your silence.

When I talk to you, I feel
I am free from all the bondings.

I miss your touch and seeing you smile,
Words will never express,
How I long to be with you,

I will soon be making my way home
to you and I know,
You will be there, waiting for me.

6. For always...

It's not simple to explain,
How I feel for you,
As there are many mixed feelings.

Love you have created is something
That will resonate forever,
in the deepest part of me.

I sometimes wonder where I'd be,
If you hadn't came and set me free?

I love the way in peace you smile,
I love to watch you for a while,
I long to walk with you for a mile.

Sweetheart, it's you in me
All day and the night,
It feels so good, I know its right.

I cherish the time I get to stare.
For always, I wish to be there.

7. Our souls intertwine.

You are my sky,
Feelings like this I cannot deny,

Staring at you,
A hidden passion burned brightly
released in each sigh.

I love you with every breath I take,
with the each beat of my heart.

I love you with a love like no other,
My life is complete, only with you.

My soul mate, my lover, and my best friend you are
for now, forever and for always my baby you shall be.

I love you with everything that I am,
With my life full of your love.

You are the miracle that makes my life complete,
Our love grows great as our souls intertwine.

8. We.

Lies the heaven made for me,

Within your soul.

Lies the love I've always pursued,
Within your heart.

Lies all the beauty of the world,
Within your eyes.

You always took away all my fears,
With your words, from the distance.

The way you love,
Showed me that love could last.

The days I hurt you,
Just makes me want to cry.

We have been through so much,
And time just seems to fly.

You take away my insecurities,
and replace them
with the wonderful thoughts.
I lose myself in our songs,
I listen to our words all day long.

9. My senses.

I never felt this way before
You are the one, I really adore.

What I feel with you is
Sweet like the aroma of flowers and
Earth after a spring storm.

At times I cry so much,
Needing you next to me,
It hurts me very much, it kills me.

I need you in my arms,
I hate that you're too far.

I light up when we're together,
And when you're gone,
My soul disappears.

You heighten my emotions and
Awakened my senses.

10. Our loving hearts.

Each morning I wake up,
Thinking of you.

Every night I sleep,
Dreaming about us.

I remember you're not with me,
And it makes me feel blue.
I miss your smile,
I miss your touch,
My heart aches so much,
With your absence.

You're so far away from me,
Yet I can still feel you within me.

I would forget about passing time,
If I look into your eyes.

I know, the distance is through the miles,
But not between our loving hearts.

11. Come what may.

You are
Like an ocean,
Down so deep.

You are
Like a river,
That will never end.

You are
Like a song,
That goes on forever.

The sound of your voice,
The warm smile of yours,
The joy that you bring.
Forever and always,
I will love you!

When you are asleep
I will guide you being awake

I promise,
I won't leave you, come what may!

12. When you're with me.

Wandering as a lost child,
I sat there, all alone.

I believed that,
Love is painful
Until you came.

I pushed everyone hard and
Made sure nobody watched,
Until you came.

In my heart the bad memories were set,
When you stepped inside,
I pushed them away.

The darkness has vanished,
The brightness has enlarged,
Once you came.

Now, look deep into my eyes
And you'll see your name.

Now, your smile is a source of life,
I breathe when you breathe,
I laugh when you laugh,
I'm with myself,
When you're with me.

13. You're spread all over.

Let me hold you tight,
Let me hold you, firmly
And whisper in your ears.

My heart is immersed in your love,
You are filled in my solitary thoughts,
And in the every breathe I take.

I can feel the love in your smile,
You are the life of my dreams.

Just like the sky,
You're spread all over! And
You twinkle inside me like a star.

14. You broke, again!

When all I gave you was love,
Why would you make me feel the pain?

You promised me,
You promised me that
You will never leave me
And you'll never be one of them
But of course in the end
That's what, you did!

You always broke your promises
And the biggest promise, you broke again!

15. I assure.

My mighty king,
My man,

My love you are.

I don't write your name
In the sky because,
The wind may blow it away.

If I write it on the sand,
The waves may wash it away.

So, I wrote your name in my heart
I assure forever it will stay.

16. Kay and my bae.

I love you,
I miss you,
I wanna kiss you.

Hugging you tightly,
Whispering gently.

My bunny,
Funny things you do.
On the sunny day,
"Honey" you named me.

You are the kay,
You make my day,
You are my bae.

17. Beating with me.

The warmth of your lips,
The touch of your fingers,
And the feel of your heart beat,
Beating with mine.

I love the way you stare,
Your eyes, so bright and black.

The ways, you show me you care,

The way you make me so happy.

Your words are like a spark of light,
It's you that makes me feel whole.
With a gentle look, you take my hand
And light up my life.

18. In my heart.

The little desires which are hidden,
Are blossoming like the moonlight.

Whomever I see, I feel it is you
You are like a lake in the summer,
Like the sun in the winter.

Though my eyes are open,
I am still wandering in the dreams.

Your voice is like the drizzle,
Beauty is like the moon!

My eyes are lucky to see you,
The lovely words you speak
Will remain memorable forever.

I promise to protect you always,
I will forever keep you in my heart!

19. I pray to god.

Love is in the drizzle,
That makes the seedlings grow,
Your love is what keeps me alive.

Your love is what that filled
The life with colors.

The magic of your love and the happiness,
And the joy you spread is all around me.

Your eyes so full of life,
So warming and caring.

I want nobody but you,
We still have a long way to walk.

You did some magic,
I can hear the musical melodies all around.

You complete me in every way,
And I pray to god, you never go away.

20. I love you.

The first time you said "I love you too"
My heart started beating like a crazy.
My ears started ringing,
I couldn't believe what I've heard,
What I've witnessed.

You just don't know,
What you have done for me
With those three words.

That was one of those moments,
Where you completely took my breath away.

You are an angel sent from above,
You changed me from the worst to best.

I love you more than anyone,
And if you ever wonder why,
I don't know what I'd speak.

I may run out of things to say,
So I'll end by the line you already know
"I LOVE YOU" more than what I could show.

21. The distance.

Even after her kajal fades,

Her smile still stays.

There is comfort in the fact
She loves me, in disparate ways
She impacts me.

My happiness, my soul she is,
She took away my chaos.

She got a blink and a wink,
Staring at her, my cheeks tint.

The distance between us, never did matter,
For her, I can even get myself shattered.

22. My hearts maim.

I watched your every breath,
As your last breath grew closer,
'Please don't go!' I cried.

My heart continually breaking,
'Please god!' I begged.

I didn't want to believe it,
It was so cruel and not fair.

I held your beautiful face,
Then I realized that you are in peace.

You will always be in my heart,
Forever, in my thoughts.

I put on a fake smile to hide my pain,
So that no one knows, my hearts maim.

23. Thinking of you.

If only you knew,
What you have done to me.

If only you could see,
The way you destroyed my heart.

If only you could think,
How much I loved you.

If only you could realize,
The pain inside me.

Whatever I did,
I did for your sake.

Today, not only the dark night
But everything scares me,
Thinking of you.

24. Nothing to fear.

When there was no sun,
You came as the light.

When there was no moon,
You came as the twinkle.

Wishing to be with you
Sadness I feel, all day long.

Missing you is my deepest sorrow.
For my mind is full of you.

When you are here,
I have nothing to fear.

25. A rare soul.

She fights her demons,
And slays her dragons.

She pushes you away,
She loves you harder.

She is scared,
She is brave.
She feels too much,
She feels not enough.

Her voice, the precious melody
Her eyes, bright and strong.

She is dying inside,
She wouldn't let you know.

She is the gentle rain,
She is the thunder lightning,

She is the light that leads,
And an anger that forgives.

She is a contradiction, a pendulum.
She is a rare soul!

26. Mystery.

Life is too short,
Humans are hard to understand.

Things are not, what they seem,
People are not what they show.

Many have tried,
Most have failed.

The more we fail,
The more we know.

Life is strange with its
Twists and turns.

Everything seems to go wrong,
As they sometimes will.

Life is a puzzle,
The mystery, so are we.

27. You're the best.

Make someone smile today,
Sit back, relax and enjoy the music.

Be creative,
Think positive.

Speak gently,
Learn daily.

Be polite,
Help others.

Live, Love and Laugh!

It's okay, say sorry.
Smile widely and be happy,

Forgive, forget and love!
Cry and scream but,
Never give up!

Read and travel more
And most importantly
Believe that you're the best.

28. Let myself die.

I heard the footsteps,
Late in the night.

I locked up and never spoke,
I knew it would be another long night.

His ruthless and cruel words,
Tears streaming from my eyes.

My mind completely lost,
My body is beyond broken.

With his hand over my mouth,
I kept howling 'stop'.

They see me smile,
But if they only knew...

All alone I sit and cry,
I just want to let myself die.

29. I can't deny.

I love you with my heart,
I love you with my soul.

Staring into your eyes,
My dreams come true.

We fight a lot, making bends
But you are the only one
I cannot resist.

You trick me with your charm,
Make me smile all day long.

Million stars up in the sky,
Yet you shine brighter, I can't deny.

30. Cry over.

I still love you and always will,
You left and I never saw you again.

I still think about our special times,
I need you the most, I beg to god
To bring you back.

Now I listen to our songs...
Cherish all our memories.

I wake up in the morning,
And I look up to the sky
I ask the sun 'why'.

On the darkest night,
I stare up at the moon,
I wonder why he took you.

You gave me so much to remember.
And the great sorrow, to cry over.

31. The destination.

She is an angel,
She is the spark of my eye.

She spreads the melody of love with her lullaby,
She is a sweet sin that showers boons.

Oh, she is my innocent baby
My cute love,
My priceless possession!

My heart has become crazy and mad,
Slowly it has taught how to love
To the one who never was in love!

As the traveler finds the destination,
I have found her.

32. My Last Wish.

When I looked at you for the first time,
You gave me an instant smile.
Everything around me was filled with glory,
I didn't know why I was so lost
Gazing at you, you were alluring!

Then my heart chortled for a while,
And voiced it was my love at first sight.
I loved it every time you caught me
Looking at you as I always wanted to be
The reason for your grin,
Today, on the cold forsaken night
I wish you were here with me.
You always spoke endlessly,
Without prejudice, all we knew was
"It's eternal"
But this day, only thing I can do is
Crawling under my covers
And cry myself to sleep,
World didn't understand us till the day
We have tied the knot a year ago,
After five years of togetherness.
Far across the seashore, you have
Promised to be mine on the night of eve
My heart beats increased, my hands shivered
Time stood still, eyeballing at you
On the first day I have met you and the last
When I was holding you close and walking
Towards your final journey in the red dress
Motionless, no color hurt me so much ever again.
Oh love, I keep talking to you with a hope
That one day you will get up from
Your bed and hug me tight.
Wipe out my tears and gently whisper
'Baby, I just loved listening to you'
I wished all the jolly junctures with you
Will last for forever but you
Have left me the sizeable memories
To recall every day in life, until
I meet you again in heaven.
I have a last wish to get you back
And then I won't let you walk away.

33. My Everything.

You were. You are. You will always be.

My best friend. My boyfriend. Love of my life.
My world and my everything you are!
'Do you have any idea, how much you mean to me'? I always want to ask you this question.
The little things that make me happy are your long tight hugs, cute texts, little surprises & the deep conversations; I can never explain how I feel when you sing me our dearest songs.
When we grow old together, we will look back at the ways we argued about many things that were so insignificant and we'll laugh and understand that our love was strong enough to overcome every argument.
I just want you to know that I'm thankful that you came into my life and I will love you till the end of my day
I want to stay in bed all day and do nothing. I want to watch crazy romantic movies and cry my heart out during the pause listening to the emotional music. I sometimes want us to stay outside all day. Stay out all night. I want to find a quiet cafe, write poetry for you sitting next to you. Do things which we always wanted to do together! I want to take care of you, all our life.

Me to you,
You to me.

You are that one person with whom I can share anything with. You glide like a dream in my heart
I would curse myself if I'm not able to frankly express any of my feelings with you.

Though I'm in the crowd,
I still feel alone.
Because of your absence!

I always have so many stories to tell you, who is going to listen to them if you don't? They say that a relationship is the best in the beginning but soon, the love fades away.
Oh. But that's not true. I fall in love with you all over again and again every day. I love you more than yesterday but less than tomorrow.

The magic of love make my heart thump
And I fly high in the sky.

Is it the friendship of smiles or
Is it the fragrance of forever love?

Do you know, where is the place that is pleasant than the peaceful? I would say it's the path we walk.
Even when it was my fault, you apologize to me. I annoy you a lot; at times I fight with you over little things. You always seem to understand when I've had a bad day. It's amazing, when you show interest in the little things about me. You are not just being my boyfriend, my love but my best friend. My heart says I'm nothing but you!
Its unforgettable memories in the heart! I would be with myself if you are with me without you nothing goes right with me!
Nothing in this beautiful world is more important to me than you, my love.

In the sunshine, in rain
In the happiness & sorrow
We were,
We are,
We will,
Always be together.

When it comes to US, **"Forever is the only word"**

34. Someday . . . You realize.

Someday, you realize how deeply she loved you for who you are. How she used to make you chuckle, smile and laugh until you had tears in your bright eyes, which now are dull and lifeless without her presence in your life.
Today you lost all the hope in your life. Once upon a time, she was there with you to conquer your negative thoughts. She made sure that you feel good always.
Do you remember the words she spoke to you? Even in the silence, she used to speak to you in the thousand different ways.
Once she said 'You are the star in my eyes' And today, when you look up at the sky, all the stars remind you of her and the words she spoke with so much of love in enthusiastic voice with you.
Maybe, someday you realize how perfect she was. One day, you may realize that she truly cared for you, loved you and only you. You were the

only one she talked to all day long yet she longed to hear your voice, missed you always.
She refused to give up on you, when you asked her to move on; she cried and cried until there were no tears left in her eyes. Oh! Why did you do that?
No matter how much you pushed her away, she always came back to you. No, it's not because she was weak. Not because of any reasons which you thought then but for the reasons which you probably think of today. And now, it's too late.
Do you remember all the words she spoke and the things that she has done for you? How good she really was! To be honest, there was nothing wrong with her. She only loved you more. More and more by each passing moment of life.
Do you know how much she always believed in you? Oh she did, more than you could ever possibly understand. She never asked you for anything. You always heard her saying 'I have you & that's enough for me.' Her eyes got all excited to see you, her voice sent shivers down to your spine. Though you were the most annoying person at times, you were adored the most by her. She said corny things and that made you smile for a while. Yes, she got mad on you. A lot! But now, you realized that she was only worried. She told you about her day in detail, she talked to you for hours, she spoke to you about many things, about her favorite book for a minute and then, how boring her day really was without you.
She was always there for you, all the time so you don't forget how much you mean to her. But sadly, one day you forgot. Many things! The little things that she did for you with broad smiles.

She is the light that leads
And an anger that forgives.

She waited for you to talk when you were busy, yes; maybe she had hurt you a little with her words or by avoiding you for an hour. But you know, right? She cared!
Many times, she went to sleep sick to her stomach and cried all night. On the following day, she messaged you first as always but there was some change in her behavior. She said nothing to you but you understood. Emojis were missing next to her texts. You knew how crazily she loved those cute hairless emojis. You were the only one that made everything better in her life. But one day, you left! You wanted to escape; you stopped saying the things which mattered the most for her. Which were

required and needed on the worst days, she longed to hear those three words from you every single day. But you said nothing. You lost all the interest, all of a sudden or maybe slowly. Maybe!

No, you were not avoiding her or said 'I hate you' but there was something missing which she knew because she was the only person who knew you. The real you! Your secrets, plans and the worst side of you. Yet she didn't leave you. She never wanted too.

Minutes, hours and days passed by. You stopped expressing your feelings, stopped talking about your day with her, or maybe there was no love to express and nothing to share? Why! Why did you change yourself? Was it for your good?

You left her alone, many times! She was bored. She was depressed. but it was all okay. She managed, she forgave you always. But never in her wildest of dreams had she thought that you would leave her alone, forever!

When things go wrong, as they sometimes will. She always said sorry, she talked to you, she discussed, she cried, she changed herself, she made you right when you were not, she helped you every time. When you needed her the most, she was always there for you. And made you smile broadly when you were feeling worst.

You were a very different guy, you were not a bit close to her in many things. She had her own favorite colors, her own favorite TV shows, and her own life. And then you came into her life. You changed everything. So much has changed in her life. Her favorite color has changed, she started loving all the things you love the most on this earth.

She never expected to fall in love with you. But as days passed by she raised in love with you only to fall again.

Yes, there were days, when she called you and you do not pick the call; one day, when you were ill she wasn't not there to take care of you; most of the nights, when she cried until her eyes were empty, you were not there to give your shoulder and wipe her tears.

Didn't she give you the best in life? Just think, think about her for a while! You realize so many things that she did for you. She changed you, got the best out of you, she always understood you, if not always then yes, most of the times she did and you realize it someday. Maybe, you did.

She is 'A Rare Soul', which you realized once she left.

People like her are difficult to find. Hold on to them! If you have someone like her, cherish & never let them go, don't take them for granted. Love, Love from the bottom of your heart!

35. Depression, Positivity & Life

There are all kinds of reasons why so many people in the world are depressed, sad or scared.
According to one of the surveys done, around three children in each school classroom are experiencing some form of mental health problem. Between 1 in every 12 and 1 in 15 children and young people deliberately self-harm.
There has been a big increase in the number of young people being admitted to hospital because of self-harm. Over the last ten years this figure has increased a lot.
As per the research, most adults with mental health problems first experienced problems in childhood. Less than half were treated appropriately at the same time.
72% of children in care have behavioral or emotional problems - these are some of the most vulnerable people in our society. Most of them want someone to give them the hope for the better future, a good life and a person to greet with a happy smile on the face with a positive mind.
95% of imprisoned young offenders have a mental health problem. Many of them are struggling with more than one problem.
If some very bad things have happened to us, we will probably think that bad things will happen again. If people have hurt us in the past, we may probably be scared that it might happen again. Sometimes, some people get so sad or scared that they need help. We may get so sad or scared that it changes the way our brains work. We may sometimes ask doctors to help us but this doesn't really work very well for most of the people.
We should try to help ourselves by understanding why the bad things that happen to us can make us feel sad and scared. We need to talk to people who are into the depression and find it really tough to get out of it. We need to talk to try to help them understand that they can do lots of things to help themselves. We need to help them understand that they can think about the world in so many different ways. We, human beings don't always need an intelligent mind that speaks, but a patient heart that listens. Supportive relationships are very much needed. Know that, the small acts of kindness can be as powerful as very big donations.

Look around, look within
Be creative,
Think positive.
Speak gently,
Learn daily.

Be polite,
Help others.
Live, love and laugh &
Most importantly 'Be Kind'

Have a look around, look at other people's problems, help them overcome the issues and perhaps if you get stuck someday, somehow, for whatever reason, when you find your life stressful, try your own ways to feel better.

Always be kind and love a little more, people may try to discourage you, some may have the worst intentions about you and its okay. Sometimes, a kick motivates us better than a pat on our back.

We really do shape our lives through our thoughts. Don't let the negativity in your mind ruin your own life. Life is beautiful, problems and challenges are necessary, we need to tackle the difficulties of life. We learn to walk by falling, and sometimes even the tragedies can turn into triumphs. Always allow the hope to live in your heart!

Read, think, debate and learn. Bring hope, beauty, unity, and joy into yours and others life.

Don't always question, 'What If I fail? What If I fall?' Oh! But darling, 'What if you fly?'

For every blocked path, there is an open one. We were all messed up at some point in our life, always keep hoping for the possibilities. Make a promise to yourself, to do better.

Act to create good out of bad. Try to do what you love as often as possible. Take one step, then another. Understand that pain and problems are not permanent.

Take a break, sit back, relax and enjoy the music. Say sorry. smile more and be happy. Forgive, forget and live and most importantly be strong.

You have the right to cry and scream but never give up. Believe in yourself, you're the best. Discover the fulfillment in the acts that you do, make peace with your own self and your purpose. Refuse to let your fears hold you back.

Once you realize you don't have to prove anything to everyone in life, but to yourself, life gets easier, clearer, more enjoyable, and makes much more sense.

Have faith in your future, appreciate your own value, and maintain a positive attitude. You should never think failures as finals. What lies ahead maybe far better than anything you ever thought possible.

Success in everything is born out of struggle
Wear your passion, live your dream
Travel often, make memories
And know how to act
Happiness in life is to love and be loved truly.

You know? 'Life's best gifts are free'

36. Hey Dad.

Hey Dad, when I was a kid, as you spoke, you combed my hair with your fingers, and I always loved it when you did that. That feeling, it was way very much better than anything.
When I was a little girl, I said so much to you. Sometimes I knew it was stupid to say some things but I said it anyway.
And today, why does my mind not stop asking the questions!
I had lost all the interest in everything about my life. My heart has been ripped out of my body, when I saw you with the blood, I saw you taking your last breathe. I saw you struggling hard on the same bed where you caressed my hair.
Your hugs were my favorite. Today, I hug my pillow and imagine it's you. When you left this world, I felt the empty feeling. My legs felt weak, I kneel down on the floor and cry hard when I'm alone. I cried and cried, till my eyes were empty. I didn't just cry, I howled.
Today, I lifted my glass a little bit higher to cover more of my face, when i was with my friends in the nearby coffee shop, sipping coffee and staring at a child holding her dads fingers firmly and smiling. However, it didn't help, my body shook as I started to cry once I went back to my room.
In the hopeless moments, I decided that to end my pain. I had to end my life. When I look at our pictures, I feel dizzy, I press my feet hard on the floor to keep my balance. Everything we did together comes running into my mind.

You left, I realized a lot!

Taking the deep breathes, thinking about you, I close my eyes tightly and try to sleep. The dark ceiling looks similar to the darkness in my heart. Many times, I whisper 'Hey Dad, I love you', my voice breaking!
I never cried in front of the people, talking about you. But before speaking, whenever I had to talk about you. I always took a deep breath

because I knew that I was so close to crying and the time to run away from others. Back to my world, my room, and on to my bed or onto the terrace. Where I often sit quietly, thinking about you, about us. Sometimes, I felt like screaming!
Most of the times, my stomach eyes and the heart were hurt badly. I ended up crying about everything that went wrong. I'm going through some kind of a pain from last four and half years. On your birthday, I kept smiling at the moon and crying at the same time. Have you heard me saying, 'Hey Dad, I miss you'?
The songs I hear, the movies i watch, so many things in the world remind me of you.
Enjoying the view from the building, standing under the broad beautiful sky and opening my arms wide, I wonder, where you are!
I heard people saying that, after the death one becomes a star. Believing so, I walk up alone in the night to stare at the glowing stars and the shimmering moon. 'Hey Dad, are you there'? I question!
I'm here, in our memories shedding the tears. You left me alone and my heart is paining. The sad music reminds me of you. A person of your age reminds me of you, their smiles and the talks. I find pieces of you in many things. I remember that last look you gave me, the way you stared at me for a minute and away from the ambulance window. 'Dad, you tried hard not to cry yet you cried.' I saw the tears rolling down to your face. I walked out silently, touching your hands gently. And then, I'm the only person who knows what happened to me in those moments. Only if I could write down all my feelings, I would write it all. But I know, no words can describe the pain I felt.

'Hey Dad,' No words can ever explain how much I miss you and love you.

You went as far as you could,
Far behind the states,
Far behind the countries,
Far behind the world.
Staring at the blank hush sky,
Looking at those shining stars,
I wish, someday you will come back
To me, as my son.

37. A life together.

I want to travel, alone and with him.
I want to hug him from the behind, I want to count the brightest stars on the darkest nights with him, I want to go for a walk, I want to stare into the eyes, I want to punch gently on his chest and play with his hair, holding his hands, I want to read for him write about him.
I want to cook his favorite food; touching his cheeks gently, I want to kiss on his forehead. I want to speak my heart out and listen to his words deeply. I want to become the reason for all his beautiful smiles & laughter! I want him to enjoy the ride sitting behind me, I want him to hug me tight, stare into my eyes and speak when I'm low. I want to play the pranks and imitate all of his expressions.
I want him to be free, I want to explore this beautiful world with him! I want to talk, share, listen, think deeply, understand things, write poetry, and celebrate everyday of life with him.
I have a wish to make out after our silly fights, I have a wish to kiss him in middle of the nights, I wish to romance with him while it's raining outside. I wish to hug him tightly and kiss passionately and then smile looking at him, as if he is the only one for me. I want to hold him tight when the things go wrong and to be there to assure that 'everything is going to be fine. I want to become his strength, on the worst of days, a supporting and caring friend. I want us to be free. Free from the ego, fake smiles and the melodramatic things.
I want him to share stuff with me, to be free, to know I never judge him as I'm not the other person but the one inside him. I want him to play with my ponytail, to make fun of my floral pyjama, to irritate me all the way, to show me his silly side, to love me deeply and unconditionally. I want him to be honest, to be truthful, and to have patience when the times are tough. I wish to hold his hands in public without a second thought. I want him to look at me and then the side ways. To feel shy, the one who can bring out the best in me; the one who cannot think about leaving me when the worst arrives. I want him to elaborate that blush on my face, staring at him. I want him to hold me tight and kiss me hard!
I want to whisper in his ears, experiencing the wind coming from the ocean.
Oh! I just want us to be together, to love each other, to fight with each other & for one other. I want us, not only for all these things but truly and wholeheartedly, what I always wish for is leading a life together.

38. A look back.

Oh lady, just look back. Look back to the first day of your love. That love which you have felt, on the very first day, that feeling in your heart, those lovely words you spoke, goose bumps you've had and the endless dreams of life.
Think, think and think my lady!
Just don't stop to think. Let your mind be free to explore the beautiful old memories. Think about the songs he sang for you with his lovely voice, which you always adored the most in the world. Think about the words she wrote for u, think about the day when he first said 'I love you' think how he made you smile always.
Just wait for a moment, don't just think, and don't go on thinking, smiling, or crying with the memories. Hold on right there,
Get them back; let that spark be alive, let that baby inside you come out once again. Remind them, remind yourself the best of moments, say I love you as many times as you want too, and don't just speak them, when you do, mean those powerful words, the words which have the deeper meanings and the great feelings attached.
Oh, when we say something, when you feel those words, when you do something out of love so deeply and passionately, we will know it. She will know it.
When you speak something with him, don't say anything just out of the habit but with the unconditional love. Pure and true! As the way, you spoke on the very first day of togetherness. As the way you cherished that feeling when you got the chance to walk with her for the first time and wished that the time stops right there.
Bring that feeling back.

39. A new experience.

She has always given more than she could; she is a girl who is more than just an 'I love you'
She showered him with endless love which she has failed to receive in her own life. She showed him something so much better than she got in her life, knowing that how it feels not to be loved truly. She don't do a single thing out of any expectations, just that she knows so well how it feels to lose the true love in life. She was always there to understand, to compromise, to forgive, to learn, to teach and to explore yet crying her to sleep that night, her thoughts changed to her father.
People say the one who goes into the heaven become a star, believing so, looking at the sky and those gleaming stars.

'Are u there, dad'? She gently asked the god in the silence
Neither the god answered nor the love of her life soothed her a little in the worst of moments.
That's what life is! The life can teach us in so many different ways. Every day with a new experience.

40. Don't just happen.

Say I love you often, say it out loud! Just say it and mean it. Don't just say. Say in the ways that your better half forgets all the worries in the world, that they fall in love with you over and over again deeply, peacefully and truly.
Remember them the great moments you've both had together, love as if she is your little angle. Love him as if he is the only person you have in this entire beautiful world. Tell her that she is beautiful and powerful when she is broken from deep within and think that the life is difficult. Ask her to stare at you, lift her head up, when she is upset. Talk it all out.
Play both of your favorite songs, remind them about that first time when you made her cry as a child and trust me, she will laugh hard and make a face when you do so. Remind her often that you can do anything in the universe to have her in your life. Tell her to talk, listen to her problems, and ask her not to hold back her tears but to cry it all out holding you tight. Tell her it's perfectly okay not to be happy every second of life. And yes, tell them that you will always be there when the times are tough, when everybody else feels it difficult to handle her and it's only you, who should be there to accept her flaws, mistakes and to make her smile forever. Because that's what the love is. Being there, caring, listening and understanding.
Oh yes, just be there. And see how beautiful the things turn out to be, I believe that more than you could have ever possibly imagined or at least better than what could happen if you leave her alone during the worst.
If you can't love someone in the bad, if you can't make them happy nor smile a little when the things are worst, then don't always just expect to share the smiles. Life can be tough at times, people can be hard to handle, and things may go upside down as they sometimes will, but during every phase of life if you both can be together, make the ways to come out of the troubles and face the challenges of life together then you know? It's true.
Meant to be don't just happen!

41. The beauty.

You were always so proud about your beauty all this while but did your beauty help you to build the strong bond with your family and friends?
Did it gain you a place in your loved one's heart? I will tell you what beauty actually is, you know, being born as a girl is a beauty, growing up and getting married is a kind of beauty. When you offer your hand to help someone brings out the beauty that's inside you,
Always remember, riches are not everything in life, if that is the case
A person, who has so little won't ever be smiling and stay happy. And those, who has lots of wealth ever finds it difficult to sleep for a while peacefully.
No matter how many riches a person have, sometimes what we seek the most is a place in someone's heart. The money is needed to run the family but not to ruin and know that it is not only everything.
That person is beautiful; who tries to bring out the best in others. If you don't let others be pushed to the side, it's beautiful. If you see someone lagging behind, walking beside them is a beautiful thing. If someone is being ignored, taking the step to include them is beautiful. People who always remind others of their worth are the beautiful souls. Knowing that, it hurts when it feels like you're being forgotten and not letting the same to happen for someone is one of the beautiful thing.
Charming is that man, who educated and raised his children in the meagre salary that he earned as a watchman. Beautiful is that girl who always loved you more than you expected, who helps people, who taught you right from the wrong. A mother who bears the child in her womb for nine months and becoming a mother is beauty. That is the real beauty.

42. Yes, Men cry!

Yes, Men cry!
They feel, they can become emotional and moody, they feel sad, hurt, bad, and worst at times. They are the one who mostly hide, the one who cannot express, some may!
Not every guy is good at lying. May be, the one you will get married too don't exactly knows how to play with your hair, flirt with you or good at making the first move.

Well, hold his hands and bring his face closer to yours. Say 'I love you' to him, surprise him and take him out on a date. Tell him all the scary and beautiful bed time stories, write a beautiful poem for him, prepare a good meal and wear his favorite dress. They're meant to be loved as well.
Let him know that you love him more than anyone or anything else in the world. Sing his favorite songs, cook his favorite cuisine, hug him from the behind and caress his hair!
Let him see the weirdness which was hidden deep inside you, let him see all the sides of you. The caring, weird and the strong person in you. The baby inside u!
You may hold his hands for a while but do the things that makes your heart hold on to his, forever and thereafter.

43.The inner space.

A man with the narrower points of view, a woman with the shorter temperaments is busy cursing one other, in the sky high building, on the wider highways they roam but with no deeper feelings. They all spend more but enjoy less. They have the bigger houses but no loved ones. They have more compromises and less time. The one's who think of gaining the more knowledge of the world but have the less judgment. Some of the people have multiplied the possessions but reduced the values. Some talk pretty much but love only a little, some are having so much of hate in their little hearts.
Some are having the higher income but fewer morals. The more liberty one got, but the less true joy he experienced. Somewhere next to road, a baby has nothing to eat and someone has too much of food with less nutrition.
Most of the people in the world have conquered the outer space, but for definitely not their inner space.

Micro Tales.

1.
‘I had never hurt you.' he said!
'Yes, you just avoid and ignore me.' she replied!

2.
“I fall in love with the little things about you” She said
“Like the sound of your laughter and the way your smile forms” He added.

3.
I shall be the mother for both,
For the one who is growing inside me and
The one who cuddles in my lap.

4.
She closed her eyes and spoke to him,
In the thousand silent ways.

5.
“You don’t understand”
“I do”, she simply said with tears in her eyes!

6.
Happiness is sitting near to the window,
Watching the love birds with a cup of coffee &
Reading a book while it's raining outside.

7.
You're someone. Maybe not to him today.
But you're someone, to someone better,
To that someone who deserves something like you.

8.
Long showers,
Loud music, and
The deep thoughts.

9.
Whenever I see all the beautiful things,
When I listen to any beautiful piece of music,
When I read any lovely poem,
I can feel only you.

10.
'I never believed in love at first sight', she said
'Until I met him' she added.

11.
Words will start to fail in expressing
The feelings that we share!

12.
Don't settle down!
Life is full of surprises.

13.
The roads diverged but
Our hearts didn't.

14.
She is crying for him,
He's smiling with someone else.

15.
She still fascinated him after 60 years of togetherness,
Even when the only beautiful curve on her body is her smile.

16.
"What is the most beautiful thing in this world?" She asked
“Those memories we’ve had." He replied.

17.
"I miss you", He cried out in tears, unable to check his emotions anymore.
"I love you, too." His tears forced her to lie again.

18.
In every story one person always loves a little more than the other,
That’s when the relationship lasts.

19.
She feels everything and nothing.

20.
“What made you wait so long?" asked my friend.
"My hopes and his promises." I replied.

21.
“What is your story?”
"I did everything to stop him. He did everything to push me off.” She confessed

22.
And one day,
'You are nothing' she said, staring at him rudely
A year later,
When she had no courage to sit next to him,
Getting closer to her, looking into her eyes deeply
He smiled and said, ‘I love u'

23.
Having a fight over a dinner, they’ve slept without talking to each other
The late night cuddles were unforgettable!
24.
She adopted a baby girl at the age of 25!
She had no sanitary napkins to use when she was a girl of fourteen!

25.
The early morning sunrise,
Moonlight in middle of the night .
The twinkling stars,
The wide sky,
The beautiful flowers, trees and the sunset.

26.
Her inner most fears were ruling her world completely,
Until he came into her life!

27.
'Stop acting like a kid,'
He said, laughing out loud!

28.
I never felt so much of pain in my life; I looked deep into his eyes
They were half closed, weak and he was crying.

29.
Nothing has hurt me more than seeing
The white bed sheet covered with my dad's blood.

30.
I remained silent.
I didn't cry, I held his hand tightly and stared at him.

31.
'I don't want to lose you'
I said in the silence.

32.
My stomach eyes and the heart were hurt badly,
Everything seemed to have come to a stop.

33.
The last day with you brought back all the memories t
That we have once shared.
34.
I cried in the silence, everything looked valueless.

People, nature and the whole beautiful world.

35.
He was there, when I made my first cry.
I remember him lifting me high and
Showing me the sky.

36.
The dark thoughts would creep in, all of a sudden.
During those days, I didn't allow the hope to live in my heart.
I just always wanted to disappear.

37.
'Sadness does serve a purpose', I felt.

38.
'How can you be so happy all the time'?
She just smiled in response.

39.
Higher and higher, he raised his volume and my voice was lost.
'Why are you so unkind and rude to me?' I wanted to ask.

40.
The color of leaves on the trees fascinated me thinking about him.
The darkness has dimmed and
The brightness has enlarged.

41.
'I wish I had met you earlier' He made a comment
And then the ocean of thoughts occupied my mind.

42.
You, my sweetheart
You make me feel so beautiful.
You make me grin, you make me chuckle
When I lose all the hope.

43.
I took too long to answer him because

I was so busy dancing to the ringtone,
My heartbeat always raised a little seeing his name.

44.
My hands were trembling; millions of questions running in my mind.
'How can this happen?' I questioned myself, breaking from the inside.

45.
'I love you baby'
I whispered and took the phone into my hands,
Only to place it back in the same place.

46.
I sat on the bed and stared at the laptop screen,
I read the message again and once again then I cried
And cried till my eyes were empty.

47.
In the love,
There can be full of arguments, lonely days, crying nights, and
The guessing moments whether "it is really worth it."

48.
Everything that she did cheerfully
To bring a smile on my face was wonderful
And always displayed the great love.

49.
Since I met her, I believed that she carried an angel within herself
The one that had sent to me for some higher purpose in life.

50.
I witnessed having a warm glow of happiness from deep within
With the thoughts of being together, forever.

51.
He never gave me the support and encouragement
To do something that I always wanted.
Supportive relationships are very much needed.

52.
Most of the times, we used to talk about our future,
How life would be after the marriage and being with each other forever.

53.
It was late in the night;
Buildings are illuminated with earthen lamps, candle-sticks and electric bulbs.
The city presented a bright and colorful sight.
I looked up at the sky,
"I miss you dad, I don't know what else is there to say."
The moon glittered and the stars in the sky sparkled brightly.

54.
Character is important,
Not the skin color.

55.
Some words are left unsaid,
Some things are left undone.

56.
Me to you,
You to me,
We, to the world!

57.
"Please listen to me, I'm sorry" he said
'Move on'
She reminded him his own words and crossed the road.

58.
He kicked her from the inside
And then she giggled, caressing her tummy.
Motherhood is priceless!

59.
They continued to talk, staring at the glasses before them to avoid the eye contact

Spending a night with a person whom we hardly know can be difficult, pretty much!

60.
Miles and miles apart
Yet close to each other's soul
She was so lonely and scared.

61.
Looking up at the sky
'God, where did I go wrong?'
She heard nothing but the silence filled all around her.

62.
She sleeps not more than three hours,
Staring at the ceiling has become her daily habit!

63.
She entered into the classroom, a year later with her head completely shaved off
'Cancer' she heard her dad saying to mom a year before!

64.
Like an idiot, she continued to talk and smile
Though pain has signed her heart and sparked a fire of memories inside her!

65.
He placed his hands on her stomach
It was the best feeling in the world for them
And to a baby who was punching her gently, making her giggle!

66.
She couldn't pretend to be cheerful anymore,
Then, she cried and cried till her eyes were empty!

67.
'It's okay!'
I tried to tell myself once again,

Probably for the hundredth time and obviously it didn't work!

68.
Her hands twitching and knees jiggled,
She felt lost in her luxurious surroundings.

69.
'Do you have any idea, how much you mean to me'?
He just nodded his head
I looked around and the last thing I wanted was anyone noticing me slap him hard!

70.
His eyes,
His dreamy puppy dog eyes continued to look at her
She saw him and wondered if she could speak something romantic!

71.
The pain signed her heart everyday and she found it difficult to hold back tears,
The one she held fingers on the way to the school left her all alone.
Three and half years have passed with a great difficulty!

72.
The house felt warm and bright,
She dimmed the lights and turned up the music.
However, that only made her miss him more by each passing second and her mind just couldn't focus

73.
The little things that makes her happy are,
The long hugs,
The cute texts,
The little surprises and
The deep conversations.
Accepting her weirdness,
Singing her dearest song.
And preparing her favorite food!

74.
With the sunset in the eyes,
Over a Coffee they met.

75.
Shine like never before each day,
And let the world see what you can do!

76.
She wore a orange sari and had a harmonious voice,
It was hard not to be crimsoned by her splendid beauty.

77.
From the day, they were conjoined
They were there for one other,
Every time they required each other!
78.
She didn't even observe how she was twitching with fury
Clenching her fists and yelling,
Her emotions were ruling her completely.

79.
'Dowry is a social evil' Kumar wrote the bright essay and has won the competition
Three years later, he demanded the dowry of five million.
- Execution is essential.

80.
The true felicity is an inner quality,
A state and peace of mind!

81.
Oh love; you are the apple of my eyes,
And the solution to all my problems,
You are the most eternal creation of god!

82.
She saw him for the first time today;
He gave her a broad smile with tears running down his face
'Three years', it was worth the wait!

83.
Somewhere, a lady is fighting for her rights
And the young man, wanted to marry just for the desire for money!

84.
Small things were always meant allot for them
Long texts and tight hugs,
Sharing smiles and holding hands,
Remembering the little things,
And those kisses on the forehead.

85.
I let out a deep breath and spoke as calm as possible
May be 'I don’t deserve you, and your love'
'What?' she said,
Fork almost fell out of her hands.

86.
'How is my new dress?' she asked
‘Nice’ he said in a muted voice, looking away
She had known him long enough; two years and a month, to be precise
To figure out he was upset.

87.
Twins cried,
But only for a while!
88.
A pat on the back,
The gossips continued behind!

89.
Early in the morning
They cried for the first time.

90.
Once she has started to do, what he has done
He understood a little.

91.

The worst past he had
He didn't knew, the best was waiting for him!

92.
She left,
He never asked her to stay!

93.
"Are you angry?"
Oh please, watch your language!

94.
"Are you feeling sad?"
Oh beautiful, a smile looks gorgeous on you!

95.
'Money can't buy the happiness' they say
Someone, somewhere down to the bridge is sleeping having no money to buy the food.

96.
In middle of the night, candy replied her.
Her favorite doll!

97.
'It's the inner beauty that counts' he said
A blind child smiled, hugging him tightly.

98.
A kiss from the success,
Half of her friends were lost!

99.
The stinging phase in life is when,
The temporary ones no longer scare you
But the permanent ones do.

100.
A moment in your arms,

Turns my world into heaven.
A sweet smile on your face,
Gives me the eternal happiness.

101.
With the shadow of the setting sun
Glowing on her cheeks, she blushed.

102.
The eyes brimming
With the unspoken words,
The coffee left untouched,
And the silence fell.

103.
He is a juggler
And she, a sloth!

104.
She gets angry on him and then she says sorry within minutes
Weird she is,
So is the love!

105.
The silence,
The fake smiles,
And the hushed screams.

106.
The silence was deafening,
And eventually sleep waded her

107.
One big house,
Twenty fake smiles!

108.
The harder she tried,
The more difficult it was for her!

107.
Hundreds of unread messages,
Yet she waited for the one from him!

108.
They were divided by the distance!
That gave her a reason to love harder,
For him, to separate.

109.
The silence all around,
The screams from deep within.

110.
'Get lost'
'Come back', he begged her!

111.
Always gentle with her words,
Bold, by her actions.

112.
'Shut up' she said and continued to eat,
A huge smile formed on his face!

113.
Late night parties,
And the early morning prayers.

114.
'Who is he for you'?
'My life' she replied back promptly. Blushing!

115.
A long wait,
They finally hugged and
The patience smiled.

116.
He left,

She cried.

117.
'Don't laugh' I said to her
Suppressing my own smile.

118.
The dark room, and
The lively thoughts.

119.
'You are the worst thing that ever happened in my life' he said
Taking a deep breath, she smiled with tears in her eyes.

120.
The big cars and
The large rooms.
The Luxury lifestyle,
Yet she chooses to serve the poor.

121.
'You don't understand'
I wanted to shout, but didn't.

122.
'You have a beautiful smile' they say
'I fake.'
123.
It's too hard to stay, and
Too difficult to leave!

124.
My eyes welled up but I never wanted to cry
'I love you' I said once again, my voice breaking!
I could tell my words didn't convince him, anyhow.

125.
'I'm sorry' she said
And then, he forgot about the pain she caused him!

126.
DJ lights,
And the darling was dancing inside!
'Happy new year' he whispered and nuzzled her tummy.

127.
The Valentine Week:
'Rose?'
'Uh?' she said and turned back
'Will you marry me?' he took out the chocolate and a teddy
On the propose day, they've made a promise to stay with each other forever.
Their first long and tight hug was followed by the kiss, which was lasted for a minute.
While walking in the garden, holding his trembling fingers & taking a deep breathe
'I love u' she said
He took her hands close to his chest and blushed even harder
Valentine's day it was.

128.
Their first kiss:
Taking a deep breath, he got closer to her
'Have you ever kissed anyone?' she questioned
'I kissed' he said and smiled at her
Before she could speak
'You' in my dreams.' he added.

129.
'Maggi' her name,
His little angel she is.

130.
He wanted to step back,
She ran up to him and smiled!

131.
Sitting in the same room, he texted her and
Ignoring the messages, she walked inside the kitchen.

The modern life!

132.
Throwing the rocks into the sea,
She smiled widely.
Sitting somewhere far across the seashore,
He was crying quietly.

133.
He promised her a forever,
Stayed for a month!

134.
Diwali:
Oh superior divine
Take me from fictitious to the factual
Take me from the gloom of ignorance to
The illumination of wisdom
And take me from iniquity to integrity.

135.
Years has passed by, they understood
Triumph comes from a struggle
Rapture blossoms from aches
When his fingers caressed her appealing fist!

136.
She wore her cerise gown
Sat idle, craving he was around
On the night of anniversary.
The perfect couples are just not
In the perfect situation.

137.
Nine years ago was a great day,
I want to mess your hair today
And I hope, this irritates you all the way.

138.
You are the great beauty with the depth of insight

Your patience and the smiles,
Have given the meaning to our life.

139.
They knew how the world would probably see them but the thing is that they don't care anymore
However, a cherubic baby boy and the girl lost their lives betwixt ferocious parents

140.
All of a sudden, she wanted to write once again
To erase the silent screams
Sitting next to the orange colored wall!

141.
Riding through the memory lane with you,
Flipping through our old photographs,
Watching an old motion picture together,
Preparing a cuisine for us is all I want.

142.
Happiness is the moment with someone who is close to your heart.
Greatest delight in life is having someone who loves you for the lifetime!

143.
Though she is thousand miles away from him,
She is the only one, who can always make him feel better.

144.
Her magnificent eyes were searching for someone special in the classroom
Then, came the news saying
'Holidays for the next three days'
She smiled broadly, having no idea what the reason is!

145.
'Who the hell made that stupid thumb up Emojis'?
'What the hell that thumbs up supposed to mean, which you had sent me last night for several times'?
Lost in the thoughts, he didn't reply her back.

'Sometimes, you ask the most stupid questions' he just thought and gave her a broad flighty smile
And that's when, she laughed out loud with an understanding nod.

146.
The opulent cars, driving by maniac males
On the boulevard
A needy girl impetrating down on the roadway
Desperate humans, varied lifestyle, fallacious feelings
Everything ends in ones death

147.
The lakhs of memories,
Thousands of blagues,
Hundreds of wisecracks,
They were best friends,
Until the night of brawl!

148.
'Stop crying' he said in a loud voice
And then, she cried a little more turning on the other side, hiding herself from him!

149.
'Winter is my favorite season.' He said, shivering
She smiled and blushed for a while, getting closer to him

150.
And on the night of New Year
He made her pout,
Clicking a selfie with him was never so fun!

151.
She passed a tissue towards me and faked a smile to make me feel better
And I exchanged the same.
That was very much missed and needed the most.

152.
The selfsame old image
Hanging on the wall

Memories were vividly abiding
They were back to strangers!

153.
A female imploring to rescue her life,
Senior male, trembling on his love seat
Struggling for his being!

154.
The rain has been engulfed on their window,
Without her existence, everything was felt as nothing.

155.
Eating in the silence, they were wondering if that day was just a dream
They remained quiet and tears welled up in their eyes.
It was worth the wait!

156.
The air seems to be so pure,
Yet I find myself breathless.
All alone in a dark room torn apart,
The loneliness has broken me down.

157.
I wished for a magic,
Under the skyline
The moon lost its gleam,
And told me to watch him

158.
Their eyes were brimming,
With the unspoken words
The ice cream left untouched,
And a silence fell

159.
The sway in your words
The twinkle in your sight
Those deranged minute fights

160.
She spoke in the language he doesn't understand,
Her childlike smile said it all!

161.
'Smoking kills'
He read and discovered all of the ways he can enjoy.

162.
He was on the world tour,
In his dreams!

163.
I like weird people
The loners, the lost and the forgotten,
More often than not these people have the most beautiful soul.
164.
We're surviving in the random world.

165.
No matter what,
She just smiles and continues to write.

166.
The early morning meditation was blissful than the late night party!

167.
He's a closed book!

168.
The writers are the deep thinkers,
To write, you need the courage.

169.
He is still waiting for her phone call.

170.
It was not really easy for them!

171.
She is uncomfortably close to him.

172.
That look on his face, when his darling smiles!

173.
Serenity begins with a grin.

174.
In the last, we always regret the chances we didn't take, the love we didn't accept, the dreams we don't fight for and the words we didn't say.

175.
She simply didn't care anymore!

176.
They truly felt!

177.
Before he could escape, I left the place first
Because, I could never see him walking away from me.

178.
"i can't imagine what you did." He muttered and walked away from her

179.
As he spoke loudly, he watched several heads turn in their direction,
His mind was racing in a million directions with the endless thoughts.

180.
We were silent for a moment
And that's all.

181.
Her thoughts were interrupted by the phone beep; she turned on the other side and noticed a girl playing with her dad.
She smiled to herself, staring at the dark blue sky.

182.
I curled my body around the phone as I waited for his response.
But I never received any.

183.
I always wanted to dedicate all of my stories to HIM!

184.
I found myself thinking about her,
All the time!

185.
She was talking, with her eyes locking with mine
I couldn't talk anymore.

186.
He rubbed my arm lovingly,
That's all I needed the most in that moment.

187.
I wasn't sure how to move on without her,
Years later, I still miss her the most.

188.
She was sitting in her dark room,
Tears flowing hotly down her cheeks.

189.
She came inside the mall with such a bubbly smile,
But I could tell that she was quite nervous like me.
After all, it was the moment we were waiting for the most.

190.
No matter what,
She always wore a smile on her face.

191.
We hugged for several moments,
I'll always remember how you took my breath away the first time.

192.
'Didn't u love me ever?'
Before I could ask, he left!

193.
Sometimes all we need is a patient heart that listens.

194.
His mouth fell open; it stayed like that for the few seconds.
Before he spoke again, one deliberate word at a time!

195.
She arrived,
His face lit up!

196.
I said something to him,
I regretted saying it the next moment!
I had no choice, but to leave the place.

197.
I felt dizzy; I pressed my feet hard on the floor to keep my balance.
It was the worst moment of my life.

198.
Those awkward silences between us lead to many interesting things.

199.
The thing that annoyed me the most about him is,
His silence!

200.
The learning takes energy, passion and the burning desire.

201.
Unfortunately, we haven't learned from the history, we only memorize the historical dates and names not the lessons, for many people school and college are the end and not the beginning.

202.

Most of her words didn't make any sense but
They were too long and that is what generally matters.

203.
He is the kind of a guy,
Who gets on your nerves in the first few times you meet.

204.
'I hate you'
He said, without a touch of sadness or regret.

205.
She is dying from deep within.

206.
I was experiencing the hormonal overdrive after
The long and expensive day!

207.
So many emotions and
Endless tears!

208.
They spent sleepless nights, yakking on the phone
How can she forget so easily and move on without him.

209.
He was sincere, intelligent and unbelievably soft spoken!

210.
I always feel,
There is something inherently good about him!

211.
'Is money everything?' Someone questioned.
'No, but we need money for almost everything!'

212.

Soft skinned face,
With so much of hatred inside.

213.
Finding it difficult to speak, he said
"I love you"

214.
Before it's too late, know the value and appreciate
Always remember, words once spoken can't be retrieved

215.
He lost her and then,
Appreciated!

216.
Dare,
Let's connect everything to a fact that we will die one day.

217.
Mostly, how I see myself is most important to me,
Caring too much about people depresses badly!

218.
When it comes to him,
She is an emotional soul!

219.
She was smiling and blushing like a child,
Whose secret is out!

220.
Natural surroundings are the best or
Even a quiet peaceful room.

221.
Being a writer,
I spent half of my life writing about us and
If I were a painter,
I could draw a picture of our story today as

It is all still so vivid in my mind!

222.
I felt as if,
Maybe, I should run away from him while I still had a chance.

223.
The German surgeons used their skills on him,
But nothing actually worked out for good.

224.
Love is what makes
the life a little easier.

225.
I feel, there is nothing worse than running away from our fears
As it leads to a road that never ends!

226.
He just looked deep into my eyes but
Said nothing!

227.
That moment, I saw her
I realized, I had never been much happier in my whole life.

228.
He arrived.
The house felt like a home!

229.
When he met her,
His big eyes seemed even bigger!

230.
My heart sank!
Because of him.

231.

"I want to breakup"
He said, his face blank!

232.
That feeling with her,
It was way very much better than anything I has seen or imagined!

233.
I lost the track of time space and orientation,
I signaled her to bring her face closer to mine!

234.
We met, and
Didn't exchange a word!

235.
God didn't seem to answer any of my prayers.

236.
Her jubilant expressions caught my attention and
I couldn't look away.

237.
When I was next to her,
She had this look of intense happiness,
That moved me into happy tears.

238.
I always feel,
The pain might not be so great, if she was around.

239.
I didn't ever tell her, the depth of my feelings and
I regret it today.

240.
She always talks to me in a warm and reassuring tone,
She talked to me about all the good things waiting for us,
That's her.

241.
The joyful glimmer in her eyes,
Makes him cheerful.

242.
She wanted to believe that he cared for her deeply,
For once!

243.
She is radiant!

244.
I didn’t speak her language, but it didn’t matter.
Her face said it all!

245.
I couldn’t imagine,
How horrible my life would be without her.

246.
When she arrived,
It was as if the Holy Spirit had filled the entire place with god’s joy.

247.
All in the hope of a scrap of emotion or validation,
He once again asked her
“Is it really over?”

248.
I gripped my phone tight, to prevent my fingers from typing again.
Because, you always said it’s over between us.

249.
I just felt,
We were good for each other.

250.
She held on his hand,
He cleared his throat to speak!

251.
She smiled a little, as he simply said,
"Let's be strong, baby"

252.
"I'm leaving" He said.
She stared at the floor, thinking!

253.
Believe that,
God will light the path.

254.
She never carries anything, that she feels,
She is not afraid to utter!

255.
I remember the hopelessness,
That I once faced!

256.
I didn't reply her back,
Instead I was just lost deep in her thoughts.

257
Tears rolled down her cheeks as she closed the pages of diary,
Ten joyful years later.

258
Listening to something unexpected may
Make us view someone in a new way.
Be careful!

259.
Her life has taken an unexpected turn,
Rising in love with him is the best!

260.
His words giggled,

Showing the boys mischief!

261.
A writer,
The one who never retires!

262.
I remember the day,
When I first saw you,
Your face, which is imprinted on the nerves of my brain!

263.
This year, he didn't wish her through a message or a phone call,
But has travelled for thousand km on the cold winter night!
He once again made her feel, the long wait was worthwhile.

264.
Five missed calls from her,
And the sixth was from the hospital.
A minute can change the life!

265.
Recollecting her words,
He cried a bit loudly once again!

266.
The one, who make you angry, is usually
The one who you love the most and who loves you!

267.
In the world, where everyone is overexposed,
He always keeps their photograph in his wallet!

268.
There is a lot of difference between
'I love you too' and 'I love you more'

269.
I'm sorry' he said, looking down.
His eyes wide open.

I noticed the silky smooth curls on his head!

270.
One of the most annoying things in the world is that
When it says 'typing' but then vanishes suddenly.

271.
She spoke with such a passion in her eyes that
No words were needed for her!

272.
Some peaceful time and deep talks has created
All the magic between them!

273.
Her silence was much more meaningful,
When he failed to understand her words!

274.
Every time he looked into her eyes,
They had some kind of a spark in them.
Shining brightly!

275.
'There shouldn't be any more pointless discussions and arguments with him'
She said to herself in middle of the night for several times.

276.
His silence did something which,
She had expected to happen only with the words!

277.
She kept silent and didn't meet his eyes,
After a minute of stunned silence, she spoke in an emotional voice!

278.
He cared so little and had
No deep feeling about her!

279.
Her piercing and lavish sense of style,
Stalked him like a maniac.

280.
He is cooler than the ice cube,
And sweeter than candy.

281.
She could sense his lies but little did he knew,
That she knows the truth!

282.
Sculpt your name in those gleaming stars!

283.
You're young only for a short time,
Live life to the fullest!

284.
'Once best friends now, strangers with memories'
He said, getting ready for the morning walk!

285.
She tried to remain unaffected with his words,
But finally when she saw him cry for her,
It chocked her immensely!

286.
Suddenly, she started feeling as everything was just a dream and
Nothing is true.

287.
He felt terrible and wanted to escape to his room but
She was too good to be ignored!

288.
Planting a kiss on her cheeks,
'Take care' he said

'Until we meet again.'

289.
Once again, she cried hard like a baby girl
Wrapping her hands around the pillow!

290.
Again, her eyes start to tear up that moment,
When she has to spend another day without you!

291.
The last day with her reminded me of the first day of the school,
The best and worst days of my life!

292.
Falling in love many times with the same person,
Is the best thing ever in one's life!

293.
All of a sudden, she broke down into loud sobs
And settled down on the floor until next morning.

294.
It was unspoken between them but,
The topic was understood distinctly.
The undying desires are hard to quench.

295.
True love never dies,
It only gets stronger with time.

296.
'I'm blessed to have known you in this lifetime'
Her ultimate words.

297.
Listen,
Never be too afraid to stand alone.

298.

The way he comfort and sing for her every time!

299.
I love the way we finish each other's sentences and
How you always say that I'm the only one for you!

300.
When I was broken, my aunt smiled
Trying to play a joke but it was distinctly ineffectual!

301.
Three of them did everything to fill up
The emptiness in their life,
Life had become as empty as the house.

302.
They looked slightly into each other's eyes,
As the music channel was showing the songs of boundless love.

303.
How could she forget those looks people gave her?
When she had nothing!

304.
Waving at him,
She smiled, hiding the sadness.

305.
And then, came the day to cry for him
Just to get the sight of his handsome face
To hear his enchanting voice!

306.
When purely true love strikes you
You let the bad moments go and
Say sorry without a small scale of displeasure!

307

Sitting down to the moon,
Emotions, over the horizon.

308.
She got a baby delight.
Crimson, when he gazed at her from the photograph!

309.
A smashed heart is the hard to mend!

310.
His every act with her has become the major reason,
For her unhealthy lifestyle!

311.
Wrapped in the bandages
Tucked inside a white blanket!

312.
We stepped out of the cab,
Walking hand in hand!
Stars were setting up,
Sky had been lighted up,
With so many disparate valentine colors!

313.
She went as far as she could
But made the strongest imprint in my heart, forever!

314.
Years have passed by, they understood
Triumph comes from a struggle,
Rapture blossoms from ache,
When his fingers caressed her appealing fist!

315.
My crazy soul has began to fly,
The courage has come,
Staring deep into your eyes!

316.
'Baby, I had the pleasure of meeting an angel on earth'
She smiled and slightly looked at him.

317.
'Thank you for the moments and emotions we shared'
He said and never returned.

318.
She left,
His heart ached, forever.

319.
'My hero, I know the heaven is celebrating today'
And then tears, she tried to hold back rolled down her face.

310.
She had none who said
'You can and you will' from her childhood days.
Her mobile flashed with ninety three missed calls and 187 texts,
On the day of success!

311.
One day,
She walked into his life and made him see,
Why it never worked out with anyone else!

312.
She was sitting next to him, caressing his looks.
Her head, on his shoulder and hands combined into his!

313.
He didn't shout at her or rebuke, but
His words would have been very much easier to bear than his silence.

314.
The silence and the darkness helped him to weep silently.
I noticed his eyes, which were dull and lost the life!

315.
Someone who is close to your heart,
Can't just be erased by the small little mistakes
That happens.

316.
Five years of relationship didn't matter to him,
While a family came with an offer of five million!

317.
Her eyes had a questioning look and
He sat there inert, feeling blue.

318.
All he could do is,
Staring helplessly and endlessly at her photograph.

319.
After looking from one side to the other,
Her little mouth started to struggle to speak the words properly.

320.
He didn't appreciate what he had until she was gone,
With her too, it has been the same!

321.
'I love you more'
She replied in a sunny voice and smiled along with him!

322.
He was the most wholehearted and
Unbelievably soft spoken soul she ever came across.

323.
They simply didn't call it love,
They were the couple who underwent through everything
That was meant to tear them apart.

324.

Always remember,
You should never give up on something that
You can't go a day without thinking about and
When you feel like giving up, remember
held on for so long in the first place.

325.
We get only one life,
Let's make it memorable.

326.
All that truly matters in the end is that you loved,
'The best is yet to come', she always felt!

327.
'Love' was just a word
Until, she heard it from you.

328.
It's only after someone is gone, you realize
How much you miss them.

329.
Our hearts are often broken,
By the words left unspoken.

330.
He doesn't love her the way she wanted,
But he loved her with all he has.

331.
Something is telling me,
Not to let her go.

332.
Just look into her eyes, play with her hair
Put your arms around her waist and
Laugh while kissing and let her know,
You are completely comfortable with her.

333.
He stared at her long, silky hair.
She stared at his soft eyes.

334.
It's amazing how he broke her heart, but
She still loves him with all the little pieces.

335.
A simple glance
Turned into a stare.

336.
He couldn't get her off his mind,
Probably she is supposed to be there.

337.
Let's educate others to be happy,
Let's value the things and not the price.

338.
True love doesn't come,
It has to be inside us.

339.
Not only the result but
Let's count every effort as the happiness.

340.
Their each sleepless night has a story.

341.
His heart shattering into a million pieces,
He cried harder.

342.
The memory of that day still sends shivers.
It seemed that life had conspired against me.

343.
People love her smiles,
His silence haunted her forever.

344.
They looked similar,
God and my dad.

345.
His silence and
Her smiles.

346.
She caught him staring at her,
'The moon.'

347.
He touched her soul,
Immensely!

348.
A pen, book and a bed lamp,
That's all she wanted.

349.
He caught her smiling,
Looking at him!

350.
They slept without talking to each other,
The following day they cooked a meal together.

351.
The real happiness is holding your dads finger and
Hugging your mom!

352.
One day,
Every word he spoke to her is turned into a poem.

353.
He asked god for an angel,
He sent her his daughter.

354.
They've seen me laugh, they've seen me cry.
'The four walls of my room.'

355.
It's with the heart that we can see rightly,
What is necessary is unclear to the eye.

356.
He made her his shadow, and that's when
He always found her standing close to him.

357.
Those people who choose to shine,
After all the storms they have been through.
358.
Don't ever let someone,
To get comfortable,
With disrespecting you!

359.
She and he,
They're pretending.

360.
He said so much,
By saying so little!

361.
We may remember a beautiful face for the days, but
A beautiful soul will be recalled forever.

362.
One day, he hugged me so tight that
All of my broken pieces were stuck back together.

363.
Someone looked for a pretty face, but
This will turn old one day.
The one who looks for a soft skin, remember
It will wrinkle one day. But the lucky is
The one, who found the loyal heart
That missed him every day and loved forever.

364.
He was on his knees,
With open arms, and a wide smile.

365.
I wanted to tell you something, but
I forgot what it was, when I started looking at you.

366.
'Thank you for those unfulfilled promises'
Holding her tears back, she smiled and said!

367.
If you're with a girl who keeps up her words always,
Yes! You're in the perfectly perfect bond.

368.
I think it's really a cute thing
When someone makes an effort,
To put a smile on your face.

369.
I want to be surrounded into the arms of my love,
On this chilling cold night.

370.
Teary eyes, don't always need the words,
They mostly speak a lot about themselves.

371.
"Have you ever been alone in a crowded room?"

He asked her and she understood that,
He is a lost soul.

372.
I understood that the worth of few things are realized,
Only after they jump out of our pocket.

373.
Though you leave, someday
I always want to be remembered
As the girl who always smiled.
The one who always brightened your day
Even if she couldn't brighten her own.

374.
I wish I had the guts to walk away from what we had.
But I can't because I know you won't come after me,
And that's what hurts me the most. So much that
Even my body shivers to think off.

375.
We were walking in a beach,
A glorious was happening!

376.
'Eat on time and don't stay up late'
She always said

377.
Why does my mind not stop asking the questions!
Why do I think of her every minute!

378.
Love: A priceless pleasure.

379.
Whenever he spoke about her,
His cheeks went scarlet, and
His eyes, deep and fresh. Full of vigor.

380.
'I can’t wait to dance with you, in our weeding'
She said and started to giggle!

381.
‘You look so cute, when you are sleeping.’
He said, taking her hands into his.

382.
I feel, she is the most beautiful and mysterious girl.

383.
Her ear to ear smiles,
Made my day.

384.
I had lost my stamina,
Staring at her.

385.
He saw the typing notification,
Finally she was going to respond him and
The joy filled him in anticipation of her reply
If not in person, then at least on the phone he needed her the most.

386.
Each moment, when I was laughing and enjoying with her
I realized how much I screamed for such moments!

387.
You might lose your heart to someone someday.

388.
However,
Her anger didn’t last long!

389.
For them, their little daughter is always the best stress buster
NIRVANA she is!

399.
You can't ever let go of someone you love,
No matter how hard it is!

400.
Never forget the one,
Who loves you the most!

401.
Deep down to their hearts they know
'It's true and eternal.'

402.
Some feelings are too deep.

403.
The way she holds his hands and
Stare into his eyes.

404.
She noticed the smile forming on his face,
From the corner of her eyes.

405.
Finally, one day they were walking
In the city of love hand in hand, close to each other.

406.
If you love someone,
Let them know.

407.
A lost soul,
Until, I met her.

408.
Every morning,
They hit the gym together.

409.

Parenthood has changed them!

410.
Love is a mystery.

411.
That intense look,
He gives her!

412.
Sometimes,
Love is tested in the strange ways.

413.
Their ecstasy was higher below the moonlight!

414.
Rubbing her palms gently,
He kissed the mole on her left hand.

415.
The wide sky,
Bright stars and a goodnight kiss.

416.
'I love you' she said and kissed on his forehead.
The first sip of coffee, he took from her.

417.
Staring at you,
My heart skips a beat.

418.
The story of her love,
Started with him!

419.
'Sloth bear'
A nickname, he gave her.

420.
For the first time,
They met, in the sky high building.

421.
Her love,
His wealth!

422.
Someone is living for you.
Sometimes, a loving word is all one needs.

423.
He looked at her from the corner of his eyes and
Yes, she observed him in the same way.

424.
'You are crazy' she said
'Always for you' He replied.

425.
'I'm the kind of a girl; you would take home to your mom'
She said and giggled for a while.

426.
She is delightful and alluring, beyond
The poems, beyond story words and the girly descriptions.

427.
I encountered a purely veracious love with her.
428.
We were worlds apart but
Destined to be together.

429.
She blushed as an infant,
Her lips utter pink and eyes full of sparkle.

430.
She stared at me for the second time and

I was half dead by then.

431.
She smiled back at him,
She has the most beautiful smile,
Anyone could see from miles away.

432.
I felt a warm glow of happiness from deep within
He made my world seem complete!

433.
She blushed for a while reading
'Do you love someone?'
In the sixth page of her favorite book!
434.
The colorful light from the Europe skyline was enough for me to see him and
When I did so, tingles of pleasure ran up my stomach.

435.
Early morning sunset,
Four hands,
Hot coffee and smiles!

436.
Oh! I feel that all the love songs in the world are telling the story of my heart.

437.
'Didn't any girl notice how he smiles?'
She thought and smiled at him.

438.
They've emerged even closer than before because of their
Deep love and mutual respect!

439.
If she had not talked openly about her feelings as him,

The outcome might not have been such a happy one.

440.
Hold your loved ones as close as you can,
As long as you can!

441.
They met,
They bonded!

442.
Together,
Forever.

443.
"What drives you crazy?"
"Our love" He simply said with the smirk.

444.
'I love you' he said,
'I miss you' she replied back.

445.
Silence engulfed the environment but the hands touched, then
Her hands were gently wrapped around his back.
The feelings were expressed!

446.
During the sunset,
We met and melted.

447.
The young man was facing her,
His hands over his mouth and eyes filled with the joyful tears.
The woman had a beautiful diamond ring in her hand and
She was down on one knee looking up at him.

448.
The best of feeling in the world is
When we were married, on the New Year's Eve!

449.
They've called her old fashioned, as
She takes the relationship seriously.

450.
Fifty years of life together, and
As he watched, she went on her knees.

451.
Love is one of the most powerful feeling and
It can make you do the things; you could never imagine doing otherwise.

452.
Filled her favorite room in her home with the perfume he loves and the photo memories from their relationship covering the walls; love balloons flying high, made his heart skip a beat.
Turning off all the lights, the candles shone bright.
Serving his favorite foods, over the dessert she proposed "Will you marry me?"
"Yes!" he hugged her so tight, playing with her hair.

453.
He looked at her,
She was staring with a smile.

454.
No matter what the situation, no matter what kind of mood came over me,
She never failed to put a smile on my face.

455.
I don't think, you know how hard it is!
As a matter of fact, I don't think anyone knows how hard it is
To love someone who lives far away through miles
But I always knew that the distance is never between our hearts.
I was so alive in her love!

456.

Things I never thought I would pay much attention too, things like a windy afternoon, or the clouds in the shape of the popcorn or an old movie, a beautiful song and many of them.

457.
His voice is very calm and sincere.

458.
It took courage to play with her fingers.

459.
In the world full of fake joy,
They enjoyed.

460.
It will always be,
Just you and me.

461.
I love you so much,
I can make any promise.

462.
He just smiles in adoration.

463.
Trust me,
Her smile will always soothe,
A little corner of your heart.

464.
He raised his eyebrows and stared,
She nodded, understanding his intentions.

465.
When they met for the first time
She was too unsettled to sit,
Rubbing his palms together, he spoke.
First love lasted forever!

466.
She is busy talking with her eyes and
He, expressing with his words.

467.
'Look at the stars' she said,
He looked deep into her eyes.

468.
Their eyes met,
Leisurely!

469.
His ‘first' 'last' and 'forever' love
She is!

470.
You surely find a way, if you want something to workout
No matter how hard it gets.

471.
She kissed him,
With her eyes.

472.
She found that person,
Whose weirdness is compatible with hers!

473.
With the right person by your side,
You can sail through the tough times of life.

474.
She may be very angry,
But remember that it’s
Only because she loves you!

475.

"I love you."
These three words might possibly are the most powerful words one can say to the other person.
Love is one of the most wonderful feelings in the world.

476.
Knowing the art of love is arduous.

477.
The amazing thing is that,
The contentment in their love!

478.
Reunited love!

479.
There's a girl who takes relationship seriously, looking at joyful old couples gives her hope that love can last forever
She writes three long pages of love letter for him, and fakes the anger just to make him sleep. She shouts at him politely, acts weird and then reminds him of how much he mean to her.
Deep down to her heart, she knows it's true and permanent!

480.
Crazy hearts,
Flying in the heights!

481.
The new sensations,
Robbed my childish innocence.

482.
Unexpressed feelings,
Unsaid words,
Untouched lips!

483.
When everything and everyone left me,
My pen came forward and took my hand!

484.
He sat,
Watching her with a smile!

485.
It was like no one was around,
It's only us!

486.
His gaze was held with mine!

487.
And when it comes to you,
"Forever is the only word". She said
488.
He took my hands close to his chest and spoke.
That moment, I felt that he is my forever.

489.
I feel, when she enters the room,
It automatically lights up!

490.
Life will reward you for everything.
Sooner or later!

491.
Believe,
Sky is the limit!

492.
You all have a gift that
Nobody can take off from you!

493.
I feel, It's true that
The words make things happen.

494.
I wish,

I can hold you once again, firmly.

495.
She lifted her hand and slapped him hard across his cheek
'I hate you'
She left and ever came back.

496.
That feeling,
When you think that no one cares!

497.
He sensed my sad tired and devastated state
I felt the empty feeling in my heart.
My legs felt weak, I kneeled down on the road and cried!

498.
"She is not worthy of your love,"
He said to himself!

499.
Her eyes were dark and gloomy,
They had lost their brightness and appeared dull and tired.

500.
The sun shone bright, taking away a bit of the chill.
It was a wonderful day weather wise but
It felt like the worst day in the city so far.

501.
I felt like someone had kicked me in the stomach so hard!
I sat on the bed and stared at the empty closet, and then
I cried and cried till my eyes were empty!

502.
The girl who never cried in front of any started to tear up,
In front of everyone in the room!

503.
In those moments I actually believed that,

No one has suffered the emotional pain that I did!
'I have nothing left now' I always said to myself.

504.
'I just want to disappear'
She said to the girl in mirror.

505.
In the hopeless moments, I decided that to end my pain,
I had to end my life!

506.
His voice was loud enough to startle,
The two skinny girls sitting next to us!

507.
That feeling when your loved one's replies you with an "OKAY"
For your long and emotional message.

508.
Trying to fight the tears,
She faked a beautiful smile.

509.
Lost her and then,
Appreciated!

510.
She hates everyone now, because
Once she loved a person too much!

511.
She left,
He realized!
512.
He cried,
Once she left!

513.

And the next morning,
She woke up in the hospital.

514.
Taking a deep breath,
She closed her eyes!

515,
I whispered,
My voice breaking.

516.
I sat down on the sand and cried.

517.
She can handle it somehow, but
It is getting worse with fights and the silence between them.

518.
She loved,
She was lost,
She is living.

519.
I don't know, what actually had happened to me but yes, I should not have felt what I felt and I should not have said what all I said to her.

520.
Feeling cheap,
I left having no courage to look at her.

521.
And before speaking, she took a deep breath because
She knew that she was so close to crying.

522.
'I'm okay.'
She said and that's all.

523.
So many emotions and
Endless tears!

524.
She cried,
For the wrong person!
525.
Sick of crying, and
Tired of trying!

526.
She never felt so much of pain,
Every day was getting harder for her.

527.
The worst feeling is, pretending like you are okay
But breaking from the inside.

528.
She ended up crying about everything that went wrong.

529.
'I hate you'
He said, without a touch of sadness or regret

530.
And one day,
His words stopped to matter.

531.
He was waiting for her,
Since she left!

532.
She kept quiet, just to let him realize his mistakes and how can he live without her in his life.

533.
She continued to cry in the silence.

534.
I know, you heard me crying but
You just didn't care!

535.
"Don't love me too much, because it hurts only you every time' he said
Only years later, she understood that he actually meant those heartless words.

536.
Her silence was hiding,
Thousands of words!

537.
Every love story she reads, reminds her of him.

538.
She understood that,
he never understands!

539.
One day, you will be asking me to come back to you
But then, I won't!

540.
Tears started to roll down from his eyes and
Flowed down to his cheeks.

541.
Crying - Her routine!

542.
And then,
She never spoke again.

543.
She was training herself to act as a stony soul

544.
She was going through
some kind of a pain from ages!

545.
Words were dried up in her mouth
Calmly, she stood there with tears in her eyes

546.
Breakup can be very harmful!

547
Today is her birthday,
She kept smiling at the moon and crying at the same time

548.
She ruined her mood for every few minutes by staring at his 'last seen'

549.
His phone call didn't wake her up this morning,
But their memories did!

550.
Messy hair
Messy room
Messy life
Nothing mattered, when he left!

551.
Her eyes,
Screamed!

552.
Reading all of his letters,
Her eyes got wet.

553.
She lived with the scars that
She didn't choose

554.
And then, every song he heard every movie he watched,
Every moment of his life reminded him of her.

555.
'I have work, leave me alone' he said
That was enough for her to understand he is upset.

556.
The kitchen, the bed, the couch, their garden and
Everything else screamed her absence

557.
Staring at the sky and looking at the moon,
She believes that he is listening to her!

558.
She was sitting in her dark room,
Tears flowing hotly down her cheeks.

559.
I had lost all the interest in everything about my life.
I felt as if my heart has been ripped out of my body.

560.
Tears began to form again
He missed, every moment they spent together.

561.
Memories are tormenting her.

562.
His every excuse,
Killed her from the inside.

563.
'Baby' he called
Recalling the memories, in his dreams!

564.
She went to his home,
Only to find the goodbye note in his desk

565.
Enjoying the view from the hilltop,
Opening her arms wide,
She wondered where he is!

566.
'Change your attitude' He shouted.
She had nothing left to say.

567.
Compromised!

568.
She left him,
He understood the reasons, when she left the world.

569.
She spoiled their life
She believed in every rumor she heard about him.

570.
They went out on a date.
With strangers!
571.
She broke the silence between them,
Only to hear the door slam shut!

572.
He took a while to respond, because
Meeting him again would spark a fire of memories inside her!

573.
Each mistake, every pain I caused to her came running into my mind
Once she left me in the dark, all alone!

574.
'I spent sleepless nights without you by my side'
She said and curled up with the colorful pillow.

575.
Her silence was filled with the words,
She longed to speak.

576.
If we lose something we love the most in this world,
So many things stop to matter!

577.
He didn't respond to her, he just stared at her for few seconds and
With the great effort, he kept calm and spoke again!

578.
She found it hard to balance her and then burst into tears
Staring at the ceiling in the dark 'why do I cry so much these days '
She questioned herself.

579.
I was simply stunned with her behavior and at a loss for words!

580.
I felt that I should stay away from the world,
To heal my heart a little.

581.
More than ever, I felt angry, hurt and confused.
I thought, god speaks to us in so many different ways.

582.
He was addicted to the dark room and
The sad music!

583.
And then, he was dead one day!
I touched his lifeless fingers and cried more.

584.
She just shook her head,
Keeping the gaze down!

585.
'Move on' he said
'Come back' he begged her later
Both of the times, silence was her only answer.

586.
'Move on' he says today, leaving her in tears every day.
'How can I let you go?'' He asked, once upon a time.

587.
'Masked', because
The world never accepts the real face.

588.
Deeply hurt, but
Looking at him she smiled.

589.
She just didn't cry couple of tears
Screaming at the moon, she collapsed badly.

590.
She never wanted to let him go.
But today, she had too.

591.
'I'm sorry'
His only words against the hundred cruel actions.

592.
"Who are you?" He questioned, angrily
She smiled and said, "The one you ruined."

593.
I was so scared of losing you, living my life without you but

You left.

594.
The darkness came rushing and
I felt no more pain!

595.
Before I could answer, she left out in anger
I felt trapped within myself! And
My eyes began to tear up all over again.

596.
Once she left,
Everything reminded me only of her!

597.
She broke up, but
He didn't.

598.
I always truly miss the feeling of being loved.
Just for once, I want to experience.

599.
'I sacrificed.'
She said smiling a little.

600.
Your voice, and
Your memories are in my mind.

601.
To understand the mysterious smiles of her.
Look into her heart, stare through her eyes.

602.
Try to make peace,
With your broken pieces!

603.

Wandering as a lost child,
She cried.

604.
She pushed hard and made sure nobody watched,
Tried to remain relaxed and pretended nothing had happened.

605.
Life has become gloomy
I can't handle the pain! And
Without you, I'm broken!
Dying slowly, every day!

606.
She wanted to take all the pain of her heart to grave!

607.
Higher and higher, he raised his volume and
My voice was lost.

608.
I silently burnt my heart desires and
Threw those gifts in the burning fire!

609.
I'm here, in our memories shedding the tears
Facing my inner most fears!

610.
My heart is always paining,
Your sorry means nothing.

611.
He left her all alone and
She has learned to live alone!

612.
He came back,
She has moved on!

613.
He taught her,
How to live alone!

614.
And after the three years from then,
They have met somewhere far across the seashore.

615.
The sad songs remind him of her.

616.
He ignored her.
She has learned to ignore him.

617.
Only her pillow knows the amount of emotions,
She hides from the world.

618.
Her tears talk,
When she misses him so much!

619.
She always needed his shoulder to cry upon,
He was never close enough.

620.
It hurts him seeing her,
With someone else!
621.
She wondered,
If he knows what he is doing to her?

622.
Looking up at the sky,
Walking on the terrace,
Watching the beauty of nature without him next to her makes her sad.

623.
Did I just hear you saying "I hate you?"
He wanted to confirm.

624.
'I think you still love me' she said, staring at him
He just smiled.

625.
Some memories last forever.

626.
That feeling,
When a person you love the most walks away.
'Is it really easy to unlove someone?'

627.
'I could never think of breaking your heart' He said calmly
'Then, why did you?' She wanted to shout.

628.
The dark chocolate she ate,
Matched to her soul!

629.
She didn't talk ever again,
He had really hurt her from the deep within.

630.
She looked at the stars, and
They shined brightly.

631.
The deeper breath, and
The racing hearts!

632.

She listened to the words,
She is afraid to say.

633.
After the breakup,
She has slowly parted away from the family and friends.

634.
Sometimes,
I felt like screaming!

635.
I hated it.
I was overwhelmed,
Mentally, emotionally and physically!

636.
A loved one died,
A job is lost.
An illness strikes,
An accident occurred.
Misfortune never comes alone.

637.
The time flew by, and
Her feelings were paralyzed.

638.
My mind urged to wipe her name away but
The heart still in love, does not obey.

639.
The dark ceiling always looked similar to the darkness in my heart,
Once he left.

640.
She cocked an eyebrow at him,
Lips twitched to make a lazy smile.

641.

He looked at her for once and then the sideways,
That's what, made her cry.

642.
Maybe, somewhere someday
He will meet her again.

643.
'Stomach pain' she said
Heartache it is!

644.
Listening to his heartbeat,
I cried even more.
645.
The last word "fine" had the loudest volume.
His eyes turned moist and her long fingers trembled.

646.
She cried, because
She loved and cared.

647.
The dark wrinkles,
Below the bright eyes.

648.
Her love,
So strong and so pure.

649.
Maybe, she has grown up as a person.
But deep inside, she is still the same stupid innocent little kid,
Whom someone can fool with their fake smiles.

650.
They were young and in love,
Fifty years later, they're still in love
And their hearts will always remain young.
651.

My mama say,
'I ruined her life'
She said and started to cry.

652.
There's so much that I heard from the people I loved the most, so many bad words.
That's the reason; I'm mostly scared to speak in the fear of ruining some more lives.

653.
I wish there was a word to describe,
What I feel for you.

654.
Far from the top a distant hill,
I could see the sky and earth kissing each other.
But never I and she were closer enough.

655.
After all,
She is my joy and the pain.

656.
Leaving the darkest thoughts,
Resting her head on him, she smiled.
657.
Drenched in rain,
The emotions were all wet.

658.
With dry and forlorn nightmares,
She cried!

659.
Time flies,
Either good or bad!

660.
The old city, and
New memories!

661.
Months of waiting,
Patience smiled!

662.
The joy of being someone's happiness is priceless.

663.
Green! Pink! White!
That's the wardrobe dilemma before going to the work.
Blue and Orange solved the problem,
His favorite!

664.
That moment when you smell the end of a journey,
The fragrance of old beginning sprinkled all around.

665.
After a point,
We can't be broken further.
Everything has a limit!

666.
And their days start with
"Good Nights"

667.
The toothless giggles are priceless.

668.
Park your ego aside,
On the lane of love!

669.
She left,
Insomnia was hitting him hard.

670.
The happiness is, being back to a place
Your heart belongs to.

671.
Now when he would return to me yet again,
I won't be the same as I used to be.

672.
You took away all of me
Leaving me in the depths of pain,
You fail to see the real me.

673.
I wish to settle in Goa, in a peaceful scenic town,
Surrounded by the old beautiful construction,
Somewhere near the sea.

674.
Remember how good she was to you?
Remember how you talked to her for the first time?
Remember the rush of blood you experienced,
When you saw her always?

675.
He often fell in love with someone,
Who never loved him!

676.
I always failed to love back,
Those who loved me.

677.
He is against molestation.
He is against all the sick acts happening in the society.
He is the one who often posts about his anger,
against the wrong act on the social networking sites.
He likes every status supporting women
But, turns a blind eye and walks away,

When he see someone in the danger.

678.
I feel, even her silence
Has a sweet voice.

679.
The negative vibes always travelled,
Faster than the Light!

680.
Before I die, I just have this one wish that
I would love to kiss her in the pouring rain.

681.
The moment she escaped,
He started to search her in him.

682.
He was paralyzed,
I wondered, what lied in store for us!

683.
There are so many possibilities in one's life.

684.
He has crippled me so badly.

685.
Who is going to preach me?
When you are gone!

686.
She just wanted to dissolve into the strength of his shoulders,
Feeling the warmth of his body, listening to his heartbeat
It had been such a long time!

687.

She started
"I was sixteen years old, when I met him"
And continued to speak.

688.
One of the most devastating experiences in the world,
Is the loss of a loved one!

689.
We can't compare anything with the feeling,
That comes from our heart.

690.
Studying her from afar, he wanted to ask her,
If she would like to give him a hug.
He wanted to just take her in his arms.

691.
She smiled and cautiously stepped towards him,
Just as she went close enough,
She stopped, looked into his eyes deeply, and
Slowly folding her arms she stared at him like a child!

692.
I can honestly say,
I'll never forget that moment.

693.
Help others, heal yourself!
Empathy is a great gift!

694.
I went back to her again,
It was like; I had no experience with fighting.

695.
Where was this moment in my life?
Until, you came to me as a miracle.

696.
She left,
The greatest thing happened to me.
To end my pain,
'Should I cry a little or should I die!'

697.
I knew still somewhere inside me,
There was a little life remaining.

698.
In those moments,
I was so touched by him,
That tears flowed down.

699.
Her attitude is always amazing.

700.
And eventually, I'd developed
A very deep fear of losing someone I loved.

701.
Whenever my teachers informed about the exams,
I couldn't walk for a day.

702.
Thinking about him,
I flipped over and pressed my forehead hard to the pillow.

703.
A little compromise is always required,
For a happy relationship!

704.
It was in the temple,
I noticed her looking at me and closing her eyes.

705.

Listening to her, 'nothing in her life would give her more pleasure than merely talking about the little kids', he thought!

706.
She was speaking in a depressed voice,
She was silent for a moment,
She knew, he had a point as well.
That's her.

707.
She looked to the pictures of her family on the wall,
That only helped her cry harder.

708.
My words,
'They have always been written based on my experiences and feelings.'
She said and smiled.

709.
People may assume that he is a serious man,
But only she knows how jovial he is.

710.
All of a sudden,
He touched on a sensitive subject and
That's what made her cry.

711.
After a long time,
He understood that, she didn't mean to hurt his feelings.

712.
She,
Such a wonder!

713.
'You shine bright like a diamond in the sky.'
She said and blushed.

714.
He always told me that,
I should focus not on what was missing, but on
What I had and what I could create.
715.
People drown in the water,
But, I'm drowning in love.

716.
Although in two different cities,
We had a candle light dinner together.

717.
Her memories won't die.
She is gone but she's actually here.
She's with me as my shadows.

718.
I never knew what love was
Until one day, I saw her!

719.
Being messy together,
Is the randomly beautiful thing!

720.
You only need the love when she goes,
Only miss her most, when she leaves.

721.
He gave me an understanding look,
Standing in the corner.

722.
Suddenly,
His face was on the fire with embarrassment!

723.
“It’s fine"

He said, disentangling my arms.
My heart stopped for a second!

724.
My breathing became fast,
I couldn't take it anymore and
I feel like I have to beg him.

725.
We stared at each other in silence for about thirty seconds,
He finally spoke again!
726.
He turned his volume down and
Spoke in a calm voice.

727.
I said something to myself,
In middle of the night!
My voice breaking,
I sucked in a breath!

728.
He must feel guilty someday,
After he see how much she care for him!

729.
For some odd reason,
She walked outside to throw the phone down the street but
Thinking twice about it, she kept it back in the pocket.

730.
When we go through a very bad heartbreak, doesn't every movie we see, each word we read seem to have a hidden message aimed at us?
Don't all the songs in the television seem to be about our very own self and our aching heart!

731.
I always found peace and comfort gazing at the mountains, watching the sunset on the beach.

732.
I think, my city is a very beautiful place but
It seemed even more beautiful when he arrived.

733.
There are some people in the world,
Who get excited about the new experiences and
I'm one among them.

734.
She left and he feared that,
His life will change for the worse.

735.
She put on a brave face most of the time,
Inside she was haunted by dark thoughts.

736.
I nearly let myself drown,
In his love.

737.
She reached to the point where she recognized,
It was time to take responsibility for her happiness.

738.
I never before spent my days and nights,
Twitching uncomfortably on the bed.
739.
Slowly and gradually,
She came to enjoy certain qualities of in herself!

740.
She is, a precious soul,
A valuable pearl.

741.
She spoke,

With her eyes closed.

742.
I realized,
Sometimes there is more to people than we first suspect and
Sometimes there is less.

743.
Support the good and
Encourage the best.

744.
She worked hard
to become, as independent as possible.

745.
I can always feel,
Her warmth and acceptance!

746.
Their distance got shortened, but
For a very small duration!

747.
Daughters are treasure to cherish and
Not a burden.

748.
We never know,
When we'll stumble into love.

749.
She looked into my eyes with the intensity,
We were silent for a moment.
The peace in her eyes took my breath away.

750.
When I saw him,
A new heartbeat came up.

751.
Tears of pain and love were
combined together.

752.
His fingers danced tantalizingly upon her thighs,
He became bolder every minute.

753.
I felt a tap on my shoulder, I turned around and it was him.
My eyes filled with tears, and suddenly
My house felt like a home.

754.
'Do you still love her?' Asked my friend
I remained silent but my heart skipped a beat!

755.
His short temper disappeared shortly but
He lost her forever!

756.
My heartbeat so high,
As if heart itself will pop out.

757.
'I left him'
She said.

758.
Don't always judge people by their past.
They learn, change and move on.

759.
Years from now, someday
You may regret doing nothing,
When you had an opportunity!

760.
I feel,
Sometimes even the god is forced to change the fate.

761.
I simply didn't care anymore,
About anything or anyone!

762.
When I met her, I knew
I truly felt.

763.
His deadly looks,
Her dead dumb brain.

764.
She said,
A very beautiful lie!

765.
Her words were as beautiful as she is
But always more tragic!

766.
She kept on loving him,
From a distance!

777.
Always remember,
Someone doesn't do something by accident for numerous times.

778.
He was genuinely astonished,
She made his world seem complete.

779.
I talk a lot but,
Only with you!

780.
Always try to understand,
The pain of someone else.

781.
Today, make a promise to yourself,
To do better!

782.
Too much fear is never good.

783.
We should do what we love,
As often as possible.

784.
Don't give up.
You will be amazed at what happens,
When you refuse to quit.

785.
Just love,
Wholeheartedly!

786.
The whole world will be with you,
If we are successful but never be blind enough
to see those very few,
who would stand by you in your worst.

787.
The one, who disrespects and leave the closed ones,
Can never be successful in the long run.

788.
My dad always said,
'With the freedom comes responsibility.'

789.
Take one step, then another.
Create a life you love.

790.
A small correction maybe all that's needed,
To experience the real happiness.

791.
Enjoy the silence and
Being with yourself!

792.
The roots were so deep, that
They never feared the wind!

793.
There are so many people in the world, who try to discourage you,
Some may always have the worst intentions about you! No matter what
Your mission then should to be patient with your goals.

794.
By learning something new,
Your enthusiasm should grow harder.

795.
Everything that happens and
Every person we meet is an experience.

796.
She finds learning more interesting,
Than being taught.

797.
For every blocked path, there is an open one.
Know that, every person was messed up at some point.

Keep hoping for the possibilities.

798.
Be a
Devoted listener.

799.
Stand up for yourself,
You are stronger and beautiful
Than you think.
Lift your head up,
Stand straight and walk proudly.

800.
She hates to go along the crowd.

801.
Birds chant after a squall,
Why shouldn't we!
802.
You are a miracle.

803.
My luck was not meant to be written,
In the heavens!

804.
804.
I went completely blank after the breakup.
I didn't know what to do and whom to talk to.

805.
He just smiled at her words and
didn't say anything.

806.
'How can you live without me?' She asked
'By dying each moment.'

807.

What they see in me is only the image,
That they have formed about me.

808.
The wind was on my face again,
I leaned back and put the pillow behind me.
‘I miss you’ I said, hoping for her response.

809.
Listening to him,
I could not believe that people could be so callous.

810.
I sat next to the window, staring at the sky
Silence and space are necessary.

811.
In the dark room,
She found comfort in his words.

812.
Holding her tight,
He smiled with pride.

813.
As she walked towards the gate,
"It’s going to be okay." He said.
814.
Kids passing on the streets,
Bring the smiles on his face.

815.
Pages of her books, brought back their memories
And she cried.

816.
When she went and stood next to to him,
He just got up from the chair and walked out of the room.

817.

I can sense him,
Waiting for me!

818.
Once again,
She woke up from a new nightmare.

819.
His closed eyes never opened.

920.
He gently wrapped his arms around me,
That moment, I wished I could stop the time.

921.
She said something romantic and
Pulled her hair back to tie them and giggled.
Those are the moments, he waited for so long.

922.
She kept quiet with him,
Forever!

923.
He noticed her hair, her eyes and
Her fingers turning the pages of the book gently.

924.
Something hurt inside me,
I felt like someone pounded my chest.

925.
We saw the kids splashing in the water at a distance,
The random thoughts circulated in my head.

926.
She said something to him,
Without making the eye contact.

927.

She tapped a foot gently to the slow beats, and
Sang for him.

928.
'No, I'm not leaving.'
He said and wiped her tears.

929.
I tossed and turned in bed all night,
My parents were not even aware that they are being offensive.

930.
The memories may fade for him, but
Their traces forever stay with her.

931.
There is no tomorrow without today, and
There is no today without yesterday.

932.
She could never figure out,
His feelings.

933.
He saw how exciting life and love can be,
because of her.

934.
He took her to the areas of pain and suffering,
And never visited again.

935.
'The wrong call.'
Said the familiar voice.

936.
'I hate you.'
Said the girl, who loved!

937.

'Who are you?'
'Your future!'

938.
'I don't care.'
'You do' her inner voice.

939.
'My dad hates me the most' a little boy said
I felt the same, until one day.

940.
Lonely night,
Colorful pen,
Blank pages, and
The beautiful memories.

941.
'Who are you?' She questioned
'The one you didn't fight for.

942.
Little did they know,
What she can do.

943.
Kids,
Toothless giggles,
First cry, and
The attempts to talk and walk.

944.
'I hate my mom' He said
I wish, I can get back my mom.

945.
'Can you drive'?
'Can we go on a long drive?' She asked at the same time.

946.

Life is short, the world is so big, there is so much out there to explore.
'Yeah, let me explore' He said and looked deep into her eyes.

947.
She was left by everyone and then
He came, only to leave.

948.
'Do you have a boyfriend?' They asked
Thinking about him,
She smiled and said 'No.'

949.
'What are you doing?'
'I'm trying to move on.'

950.
Close your eyes and
Listen to what your heart has to say to you, once.

951.
'Who are you?' He asked angrily
'The one you cheated.'

952.
The broken hearts & shattered dreams,
Quiet night and still tree.
A broken wall, locked door.
Somewhere, a lone leaf swaying.

953.
I will never get bored of this city,
I'll be waiting for you, right here.

954.
I'm here in your memories,
Waiting for you to return.
On this dark and silent night,
I wish you were here.

955.
I love airports and packing the bags,
The smell of a new city.

956.
I'm pretending like I don't miss you,
You're pretending like you don't care.

957.
She stood strong,
The wound may heal someday but
The mark they made is still deep.

958.
In love,
The deaf heard noises,
The blind saw light.

959.
Soon after the school, we lost the connection
I texted her a lot but she never replied.
I still love and need her the most.

960.
There is always a ray of hope,
amidst the darkness.

961.
She wished for his death, and
He, for her wellbeing.

962.
He never read any of her poetry,
He made her one!

963.
The soft moonlight,
The shimmering sky,
The rays of the moon, and

Bunch of sparkling stars.

964.
He dozed off,
She stared.

965.
He touched,
Her soul.

966.
I love you so much more than,
You could ever possibly know.

967.
The worst happened to her,
He left,
Parents cursed,
Yet she smiles.

968.
He came by running towards her,
Took the slow steps while returning back,
As if he is kissing the mother earth.

969.
The story of her scars,
Remained untold!

970.
He blocked the way and
Hugged her.

971.
Listening to her heartbeat,
'I love you' He said.

972.

Brutally, she cursed him
He left, smiling.

973.
'He is so lucky to have you' they said
She just smiled in response.

974.
The bright colored pictures,
But the fake smiles
Blank minds, posing all together
Hands in hands, unknown stories and
The ego battles.

975.
I was finally getting over you,
By trying to understand that,
I didn't need you.

976.
Her favorite songs and
Her favorite books,
Told me more about her.

977.
The dark sky,
Thunder, and
Your presence.

978.
Looking at her mystical beauty
Just like the sun, who makes every day bright
Her smile lights up my day.

979.
Crawling by my side on the lonely nights,

She brings the smiles with her silly fights.

980.
I love the way, he looks at me
Wherever I go, he stays with me.

981.
She made many proud with her fame,
While the cursed, bowed in shame.

982.
He may not get to see her as often as he wants,
She may not get to hold him in her arms all through the night.
But deep down to their hearts, they knew it's true.

983.
No matter what,
I truly know, you're the one that I love, and
I can't let you go.

984.
Throughout our life, we will meet one person
Who is like no other and that one is you to me.

985.
He sends me the flowers,
When I least expect it.

986.
Love is not always about
When you can't be apart from someone for too long but
If we are patient enough to wait.

987.
My love,
If you can count all the stars in the sky,
You simply will have a sample of

How much I love you.

988.
Although you may not love me,
You know that I'll be there.

989.
Don't forget that,
When your heart is broken,
You can always lean on me.

990.
He holds her tightly and
Kisses on the forehead.

991.
He grabbed her hand while walking together,
That's when, she felt the spark.

992.
Did you ever fall for someone,
You know you shouldn't? But
Your poor heart had no idea but to feel.

993.
I had fallen deeper with each passing day, but
Tried to hide it in every possible way.

994.
In my heart,
It is you and only you,
For always!

995.
That feeling,
When you look at someone and
They give you that authentic smile.

996.
As soon as I wake up,
It's your face, I see for always.
As soon as I get online,
It's your name, I look for first.

997.
You know,
What makes my heart skip a beat?
It's your name.

998.
My love,
You are always you,
That makes me want you.

999.
When she held his hand,
Diwali happened.

1000.
'Two hearts?' She asked innocently.
'One soul' He said, blushing.

A note on the author.

Jyoti Patel is currently based in Hyderabad, A student, an ardent lover of western and classical music. She enjoys reading and writing.

She is a blogger, a poetess and has been a contributing poet and author to many anthologies thus, her passion & expertise in poetry and storytelling is very much evident in her first book ***Sensation of a Soul***. She has an eye of curiosity and an inquisitive sense to explore. There was a time when she wanted to take up wildlife photography as a career. She is now currently busy working on her next book ***"Two Hearts, One Soul."***

You can email her at ***hiammu@outlook.com*** and find her on Instagram, Facebook, Google Plus and Twitter with the username ***Jyotipatelammu***.

Stay connected. Keep smiling.

Printed in Poland
by Amazon Fulfillment
Poland Sp. z o.o., Wrocław